MW00529606

in a word

Lauren Yee

A SAMUEL FRENCH ACTING EDITION

FOUNDED 1830

SAMUELFRENCH.COM
SAMUELFRENCH-LONDON.CO.UK

MUSIC USE NOTE

Licensees are solely responsible for obtaining formal written permission from copyright owners to use copyrighted music in the performance of this play and are strongly cautioned to do so. If no such permission is obtained by the licensee, then the licensee must use only original music that the licensee owns and controls. Licensees are solely responsible and liable for all music clearances and shall indemnify the copyright owners of the play(s) and their licensing agent, Samuel French, against any costs, expenses, losses and liabilities arising from the use of music by licensees. Please contact the appropriate music licensing authority in your territory for the rights to any incidental music.

IMPORTANT BILLING AND CREDIT REQUIREMENTS

If you have obtained performance rights to this title, please refer to your licensing agreement for important billing and credit requirements.

IN A WORD was first produced by San Francisco Playhouse (Bill English, artistic director, Susi Damilano, producing director) as part of a National New Play Network rolling world premiere in San Francisco, California on April 2, 2015. The performance was directed by Giovanna Sardelli, with sets by Catalina Niño, costumes by Karina Chavarin, lights by Matthew Johns, sound by Madeleine Oldham, and props by Leah Hammond. The Production Manager was Jordan Puckett and the Stage Manager was Beth Hall. The cast was as follows:

FIONA	Jessica Bates
GUY	Cassidy Brown
MAN	Greg Ayers

It was then produced by Cleveland Public Theatre (Raymond Bobgan, executive artistic director) as part of a National New Play Network rolling world premiere in Cleveland, Ohio on April 17, 2015. The performance was directed by Beth Wood, with sets by Beth Wood, costumes by Ali Garrigan, lights by Ben Gantose, sound by Sam Fisher, and props by Jacqueline Westhead. The Stage Manager was Amanda Lin Boyd. The cast was as follows:

FIONA	Liz Conway
GUY	Mark Rabin
MAN	Matt O'Shea

It was then produced by Strawdog Theatre Company (Hank Boland, artistic director) as part of a National New Play Network rolling world premiere in Chicago, Illinois on February 15, 2016. The performance was directed by Jess McLeod, sets by Sarah JHP Watkins, costumes by Izumi Inaba, lights by John Kelly, sound by Heath Hays, and props by Jamie Karas. The stage manager was Melanie Kula and the Production Manager was Emmaline Keddy-Hector. The cast was as follows:

FIONA	Mary Winn Heider
GUY	John Ferrick
MAN	Gabriel Franken

IN A WORD was first presented at University of California San Diego's Baldwin New Play Festival (Naomi Iizuka, head of playwriting) at the Arthur Wagner Theatre in La Jolla, California on April 16, 2010. The performance was directed by Adam Arian, with costumes by Sue Makkoo, lights by Sherrice Mojgani, sound by Joe Huppert, and dramaturgy by Shirley Fishman. The Stage Manager was Kelly Hardy. The cast was as follows:

FIONA . . . . Megan Robinson

GUY . . . . Kyle Anderson

MAN . . . . .Paul Scudder

IN A WORD was also developed at the Williamstown Theatre Festival, the Hangar Theatre, Aurora Theatre, Lincoln Center/LCT3, and Boston Court.

CHARACTERS

1. **FIONA** – female, 30s-40s
2. **GUY** – male, 30s-40s, Fiona's husband
3. **MAN** – male, plays multiple people:

KIDNAPPER – a guy you'd otherwise hang out with

DETECTIVE – missing persons detective

TRISTAN – seven years old, smart, different, maybe has Asperger's

PRINCIPAL – Ted, Fiona's boss

ANDY – Guy's friend, a real nice fucker

CLIENT

PHOTOGRAPHER

OFFICER – police officer on the day of the kidnapping

SETTING

Fiona and Guy's living room.

TIME

Now and two years earlier.

AUTHOR'S NOTES

In this play, objects have a life of their own. Objects come up again whether you want them to or not. Words also come up again, and sometimes the characters realize this or not. Time is very fluid.

SPECIAL THANKS

Naomi Iizuka, Adele Edling Shank, Allan Havis, Ryan Purcell, Ethan Heard, Nan Barnett, Antje Oegel, and Bailey Williams.

For my parents

Scene

(*Living room.*)

(*Lights up on* **FIONA**. *She holds a glass jar in her hands, as if she has just come across it. The jar is empty. And yet, it feels like something is inside.*)

(**FIONA** *starts to unscrew the lid. Very faint whispering is heard.*)

(*Lights up on the rest of the room.* **FIONA** *stands next to a large cardboard box filled with papers and children's sweaters. Papers and various belongings litter the floor. Behind her, a pair of glass doors leads into the backyard.*)

(**GUY** *returns home from work with a newspaper and a small paper bag.*)

GUY. Fiona, you ready?

FIONA. Mmh.

GUY. You're not ready.

FIONA. I am.

GUY. Thought you wanted to go to dinner.

FIONA. I do.

GUY. Thought you wanted to go now.

FIONA. In a minute.

GUY. It took me two months to get this reservation.

FIONA. Then another minute's not gonna hurt. I just need to find one little thing and then we'll go.

GUY. You absolutely, positively promise?

FIONA. Yes.

GUY. Okay.

*(**GUY** drops a small bag in **FIONA**'s lap.)*

GUY. Here.

FIONA. What is it?

GUY. What's brown and sticky?

FIONA. A stick.

GUY. A cupcake.

> *(**FIONA** pulls out a chocolate cupcake from the bag.)*

A little something, from Andy.

FIONA. Why?

GUY. Just to celebrate.

FIONA. Celebrate what?

GUY. I don't know. "Happy birthday," I guess?

FIONA. Oh. Right. *(beat)* Later. I'll have it later. After dinner.

> *(**FIONA** puts the cupcake away.)*

GUY. So how was your day today?

FIONA. Fine.

GUY. Anything interesting?

FIONA. Not really.

GUY. I saw, you know.

FIONA. What?

> *(**GUY** holds up his newspaper.)*

GUY. The article, in the newspaper.

FIONA. Good.

GUY. Local section, front page.

FIONA. I know.

GUY. I thought we agreed we weren't talking about this anymore. Thought you said you never wanted to talk about it again.

FIONA. They called.

They wanted to know how we were doing, two years later.

They just wanted a word.

What was I supposed to say?

GUY. "No?" That's a word. Say that.

FIONA. If it's for the case –

(*shrugs*) It was for the case.

GUY. 'Cause you know:

Andy once had a girlfriend. Who had a kid.

She stopped talking to the media. And it helped.

FIONA. Hey, you get something in the paper, and all kinds of people come out of the woodwork.

GUY. Exactly.

FIONA. Just today: I was in the grocery store and all of a sudden, out of nowhere, this guy comes right up to me and says –

(*From out of nowhere, a* **KIDNAPPER** *approaches* **FIONA**.)

KIDNAPPER. Hey.

FIONA. Hey...?

(*Flashback to earlier in the day. At the grocery store.*)

(**FIONA** *in the fruit aisle, examining melons. Next to her, a* **KIDNAPPER**.)

(**GUY** *remains in the background, listening to the story.*)

KIDNAPPER. I know you.

FIONA. Excuse me?

KIDNAPPER. In the paper. This morning? Fiona Hamlin?

FIONA. Oh. Right. Yeah.

(*The* **KIDNAPPER** *smiles, stares at* **FIONA**.)

KIDNAPPER. You don't remember me, do you?

FIONA. I'm sorry, should I?

KIDNAPPER. Think I had your kid.

FIONA. In class?

KIDNAPPER. In captivity.

FIONA. (*amused but disbelieving*) Noooo.

KIDNAPPER. I'm pretty sure.

FIONA. You got a picture?

> *(The* **KIDNAPPER** *opens his wallet, shows* **FIONA** *a picture.)*

Omigod, that's Tristan!

GUY. And what did he have to say for himself?

FIONA. Honestly, I didn't think to bring it up.

GUY. I think you imagined it.

FIONA. Guy.

GUY. I'm just saying: you met him buying watermelon?

FIONA. Cantaloupe!

GUY. And you're not the least bit suspicious.

FIONA. He came up to me.

GUY. Exactly.

FIONA. You don't believe me.

GUY. I'm just saying –

There's this guy and there was that last guy.

FIONA. Which guy?

KIDNAPPER. At the bakery.

At the school.

At the gas station.

FIONA. *(shrugs)* So I see lots of them.

GUY. They can't all be your guy.

FIONA. No?

GUY. 'Cause you know you only get one. *(beat)* Did you even ask him?

FIONA. I tried. *(to* **MAN***)* Did you hurt him?

KIDNAPPER. Did I ever?

FIONA. Did you hit him?

KIDNAPPER. Did I ever!

FIONA. What did you do with him?

KIDNAPPER. Same thing as you: I lost him.

> *(The* **KIDNAPPER** *moves to leave.)*

FIONA. *(to* KIDNAPPER*)* Wait.

KIDNAPPER. I should get going. My meter's gonna expire –

FIONA. What're you up to tomorrow?

KIDNAPPER. Listen, lady: I said hi, it's been nice, but really I gotta go.

FIONA. Where is he?

KIDNAPPER. He was right under your nose. Have a good day.

> *(The* KIDNAPPER *disappears. Back to the present and the living room.)*

GUY. So he gave you a cantaloupe?

FIONA. Which he touched. Which I then brought to the detective.

GUY. Why?

FIONA. Why not?

GUY. Because you think he's an idiot.

Because the longer he stays on this case, the worse he seems to get.

FIONA. Worse is better than nothing.

GUY. And what did you say, huh? "I met a guy and another guy and among the six of them I may have your guy?"

FIONA. I did. I do.

> *(Flashback to earlier in the day.)*

> *(The* DETECTIVE *at his desk, showing* FIONA *pictures of children.)*

DETECTIVE. How 'bout this one?

FIONA. No.

DETECTIVE. You sure?

FIONA. Yep.

DETECTIVE. And this?

FIONA. No. *(beat)* I'm sorry, Detective, but look: I came in about a lead.

(FIONA shows the DETECTIVE the KIDNAPPER's cantaloupe.)

DETECTIVE. A melon?

FIONA. A man.

(The DETECTIVE more closely evaluates the cantaloupe.)

DETECTIVE. *(confused)* A cantaloupe.

FIONA. We were in the produce aisle.

DETECTIVE. *(re: cantaloupe)* And how is this a lead?

FIONA. Well, I was talking to this man in the grocery store, and I think he might've been the one.

(The DETECTIVE cuts up the cantaloupe for eating. He takes a bite, contemplates the cantaloupe.)

DETECTIVE. So: what'd he look like?

FIONA. Six foot.*

DETECTIVE. Yep.

FIONA. Green eyes.

DETECTIVE. Sure.

FIONA. Red hair.

DETECTIVE. So: me.

FIONA. Right. No.

DETECTIVE. You get a name?

FIONA. No.

DETECTIVE. A license plate, a blood type – ?

FIONA. *(sheepish)* His meter was gonna expire.

DETECTIVE. You get anything?

FIONA. I got a cantaloupe...?

DETECTIVE. Not much of a lead.

FIONA. Sorry.

DETECTIVE. *(re: cantaloupe)* Though it *is* delicious!

---

*The following description of the KIDNAPPER should be altered to reflect the actual appearance of the actor playing the KIDNAPPER, with the most distinctive feature last.

(The **DETECTIVE** *offers a slice of cantaloupe to* **FIONA**.*)*

(re: cantaloupe) Can't escape?

FIONA. What?

DETECTIVE. Cantaloupe. Have a piece.

FIONA. No. I brought it for you. For evidence.

DETECTIVE. Eh, more than enough guilt to go around. You sure? All right...

(The **DETECTIVE** *finishes the cantaloupe by himself. He then searches for something.)*

Not to worry, Mrs. Hamlin. We may not have answers, but we always have leads.

(The **DETECTIVE** *plunks down a cardboard box. The same cardboard box* **FIONA** *was looking through at the top of the scene. Several leaves float out of the box.)*

FIONA. Leaves?

DETECTIVE. So your son, seven years old?

FIONA. Yes.

DETECTIVE. Second grade?

FIONA. *("yes")* He was in my class. I teach – *(corrects)* taught –

DETECTIVE. And kid's shirt size small, right?

FIONA. Right.

DETECTIVE. Now tell me: is he a sweater?

FIONA. What?

(The **DETECTIVE** *reaches into the box of leaves and pulls out a sweater. All of the sweaters are wrong for a seven-year-old boy. Some of them are too big, too garish. Some are girl sweaters.)*

DETECTIVE. Is he this sweater?

FIONA. No.

DETECTIVE. How 'bout this one?

FIONA. He's not a sweater –

DETECTIVE. – that you know of.

Two years, he might've faded, shrunk.

We're not looking for a perfect fit here –

FIONA. These are girl sweaters.

These are ugly sweaters.

(The **DETECTIVE** *demonstrates, feels the sweaters.)*

DETECTIVE. "Leave no rock unturned": that's what I always say. One time, lady lost her son. Fifteen years. They found him as a rock, right in her own backyard. Cold, hard, igneous. But it was him. Right under her nose. *(question)* You've checked under your nose recently.

FIONA. Yes!

DETECTIVE. Okay, okay.

FIONA. Give me something else. Give me something real. I bring you evidence –

DETECTIVE. Technically, you're bringing me cantaloupe.

FIONA. – and all you show me are rocks and leaves and, and sweaters.

You are wasting my time.

DETECTIVE. *(beat)* You're right. I am.

FIONA. No, wait.

DETECTIVE. You can go.

FIONA. Detective, please –

DETECTIVE. Listen, lady: I know this's tough, and maybe you don't think your son's a rock or a sweater or anything else like that, but whatever he once was, he isn't anymore. People come in here, looking for a missing person and sometimes it isn't gonna be a person. Sometimes it's just gonna be a sweater.

FIONA. It's fine. I'll take it.

*(***FIONA*** takes the box. The* **DETECTIVE** *exits. Back to the present with* **FIONA** *and* **GUY**.*)*

Always worth a second look, right?

I hear it takes time.

He says it takes time.

DETECTIVE. *(offstage)* And sweaters!

FIONA. He said he might swing by later. To drop something off.

GUY. Which means we should go now, right?

Before you turn this place into a real mess.

FIONA. Guy, this place is always a mess, whether it's me or not.

GUY. Fiona –

FIONA. No, seriously: you need to get that lock fixed. Sometimes I come home and the door isn't even all the way shut.

GUY. It's probably just us.

FIONA. I mean it!

GUY. No one is following you around.

FIONA. Oh really?

GUY. No one is in the corner of your eye or the back of your mind or anything else like that.

FIONA. You don't know.

GUY. I do 'cause he's not.

FIONA. Sometimes, I come in and it's like we've been robbed,

Like someone comes in when we're not here –

> *(The* **MAN** *enters with a white cardboard box and begins to steal various objects from the room. All kinds of stuff, but mainly things that could have been* **TRISTAN***'s.* **FIONA** *and* **GUY** *are unaware of him.)*

GUY. – and rearranges the furniture?

> *(Thus inspired, the* **MAN** *also rearranges the furniture for the next scene.)*

FIONA. I used to step on his toys all the time.

I used to find them at night, walking through the house.

"You don't put them away, I'm gonna throw them out.

FIONA & MAN. Take care of your things, or you're gonna lose them."

FIONA. And now?

> (**FIONA** *gestures "poof!" The* **MAN** *finishes his work. A wind blows him out of the scene, with the white box.*)

FIONA. I go into his room sometimes and it's never the same as how I left it.

GUY. I wouldn't worry about it. I'm sure it's just us.

FIONA. Sometimes I don't know.

GUY. So what're you looking for anyway?

FIONA. The box. The white box.

GUY. The box with all his toys?

FIONA. And all the pictures. The newspaper asked if I had anything else, to put on the website, so I started looking for the pictures and – nothing!

GUY. But the pictures, you have them on your laptop.

FIONA. No. I don't. All the pictures're in the white box.

GUY. Then I'm sure it'll turn up.

FIONA. Where?

GUY. Go to dinner,

   Clean up,

   Get some rest,

   And the white box will be right where you left it.

   Because you know, Andy once had a girlfriend who had a kid.

   She cleaned house and it helped.

FIONA. I don't want to do what the girlfriend Andy once had once did.

   I don't want to do what anyone Andy once did did.

GUY. All I'm saying is, I bet you'll wake up tomorrow and it'll be right where you left it. Right under your nose. Okay?

FIONA. All right...

> (**FIONA** *goes to get her shoes. Then a sudden noise.* **FIONA** *looks around.*)

FIONA. What was that?

GUY. What.

FIONA. That noise. *(beat)* You didn't hear that?

GUY. No?

FIONA. Oh.

GUY. Probably just the wind.

     (**FIONA** *looks into the backyard.*)

FIONA. I bet it's in the basement.

GUY. Fiona –

FIONA. Go look for me.

     (**GUY** *stares at the newspaper.*)

GUY. Is that why you gave them this picture?

FIONA. It's the picture we always use. It's a good picture.

GUY. It's an old picture.

FIONA. Two years go by and they're all old pictures.

GUY. From when he was two?

FIONA. It's all I could find.

GUY. What about the picture from Picture Day?

FIONA. They're with the detective. It's part of his case file.

GUY. Well, if he's coming by later. Ask him. Use those.

FIONA. Guy.

GUY. "Most recent picture?"

    That's what they said, right?

    Picture Day: you can't get any more recent than that.

FIONA. Oh come on.

GUY. Why not?

FIONA. Picture Day? People don't want to see that.

GUY. No?

FIONA. No! "Day he disappeared," how does that sound?

    It sounds morbid, that's how it sounds.

    People don't want to remember that.

    People don't want to see –

       (*Camera flash.*)

GUY. What?

     (*We segue into the past: Picture Day.*)

Scene

(Picture Day – Day of the kidnapping.)

*(**TRISTAN** squirms a bit, as **FIONA** adjusts his clothes.)*

FIONA. Picture Day!

TRISTAN. Yep.

FIONA. Tristan, are you ready?

*(**TRISTAN** groans a little.)*

I said, Tris, you ready?

TRISTAN. Yep.

FIONA. You sure?

TRISTAN. Yep.

FIONA. Okay, then: which one?

*(**FIONA** looks into the cardboard box, offers various sweaters.)*

Black and tan?

Red and white with stripes all over?

*(**TRISTAN** pulls out one sweater.)*

TRISTAN. Brown and sticky.

FIONA. What?

TRISTAN. *(chooses)* Green and blue.

FIONA. All right then.

Very nice.

Comb your hair

Fix your shirt

Tuck it in

Now give me a kiss

Give me a kiss.

*(**FIONA** gets a kiss from **TRISTAN**.)*

You look very nice. Now try to keep it that way.

Okay?

C'mon.

(FIONA tickles TRISTAN, he squirms and squeals. She smiles and kisses him on the forehead. FIONA helps TRISTAN into his sweater. Fastforward to FIONA and TRISTAN in the auditorium. TRISTAN sits in the chair. FIONA speaks to an unseen Photographer.)

FIONA. Hold on.

(to TRISTAN) Your pants are falling.

Pick up your pants, Tris, they're gonna fall down.

(TRISTAN picks up his pants, sits down in the chair.)

Eyes nice and wide now.

(The Photographer takes out a comb, combs TRISTAN's hair. TRISTAN fusses a tiny bit.)

I'm sorry. He'll be fine.

(TRISTAN holds his pose. Camera flash. We see the photograph of TRISTAN. Typical Lifetouch stuff: neat, perfect, adorable, on an abstract colored background. FIONA beams.)

(Back to the present.)

GUY. See what? People don't want to see what?

FIONA. That. It's just –

GUY. Go call him.

FIONA. Who?

GUY. The detective. Just ask him for the photos back. If you're gonna put his picture online, we might as well have the right one, don't you think?

FIONA. I'm not going to bother him again.

GUY. You want me to do it then?

(GUY picks up the home phone.)

FIONA. Guy –

GUY. If someone's gonna see something,
     They should see something correct, right?

(FIONA grabs the phone away from GUY.)

Scene

(Living room.)

*(**GUY** holds up the newspaper.)*

GUY. *(to us)* Fiona has a story and usually it contains the
words:

*(**FIONA** pulls out a set of words and reads them, as
she has read them dozens of times before, in various
orders.)*

FIONA. Love
Loved
My baby
Tristan
He was a
Is a

GUY. Twenty-four months of the same words, countless
permutations, rotating through her vocabulary, but
always the same –

FIONA. Good kid
Who we
Miss
Every
Day after day

GUY. And the funny thing is:
They're none of the words I remember her saying while
he was here.

FIONA. Blink and you
Miss him

GUY. Not a one!

FIONA. All the time
He was –

*(**GUY** adds a word of his own.)*

GUY. Difficult.

*(**FIONA** notices **GUY** for the first time.)*

FIONA. What?

GUY. Difficult. He was all those things, but he was difficult, too.

FIONA. *(faux playful)* This is my story, Guy. I'm talking. Get your own story and stop butting into mine, okay?

GUY. He was.

FIONA. *(dismissive)* Okay.

GUY. He was.

FIONA. Maybe. I don't remember.

> (**GUY** *conjures up a memory of* **TRISTAN** *in the midst of a tantrum.* **TRISTAN** *flops into a pile of leaves in the backyard, spreads them everywhere.*)

> (**FIONA** *sees* **TRISTAN** *but does not acknowledge anything wrong with this scene.*)

GUY. Doesn't sound familiar?

FIONA. I don't hear anything.

GUY. You sure?

FIONA. *(shrugs, looks off in the distance)* Is that a tree?

GUY. No.

FIONA. Then I don't know what you're talking about.

> (**TRISTAN** *enters and produces a box of dirty laundry. He takes a piece out for every secret, passes it to* **GUY**. *An unseen audience of second graders egg him on.*)

TRISTAN. She snores.

She smells.

She farts in her sleep.

She sleeps on the couch.

And she hits me.

On the lips.

GUY. None of this?

FIONA. Nope.

> (**FIONA** *exits.* **GUY** *stuffs all the laundry back into the box.*)

> *(Flashback to* **GUY** *and* **TRISTAN** *in the backyard,*
> *sharing a moment.* **GUY** *drinks an espresso.)*

GUY. Tris, you can't be doing that.

TRISTAN. Why not?

GUY. How would you like it if she brought your dirty laundry to class?

> *(***TRISTAN*** shrugs.)*

She's your mother, but she's your teacher, too, and she's been under a lot of pressure lately.

TRISTAN. 'Cause of me?

GUY. 'Cause of herself.

She's only cranky 'cause she's tired.

She's only angry 'cause she's disappointed in herself.

She's just been having a rough time.

TRISTAN. What're you having?

GUY. I'm having an espresso.

TRISTAN. I want some.

GUY. It's only for grown-ups.

TRISTAN. I'm a grown-up.

GUY. You're seven. It's only for grown-ups who're having second thoughts.

TRISTAN. I'm a second thought.

GUY. Who're having a mid-life crisis.

TRISTAN. I'm a mid-life crisis.

GUY. No, you're not.

TRISTAN. I am! I'M A FUCKING MID-LIFE CRISIS! AAAAAAAAH.

GUY. *(amused)* When you're older, you will be.

> *(***TRISTAN*** waits, then…)*

TRISTAN. I'm older.

GUY. I know.

TRISTAN. And older.

And older.

I'm older than I've ever been,
Than I'll ever be.

GUY. What?

TRISTAN. Pleeeease?

(**GUY** *hands* **TRISTAN** *his espresso.*)

GUY. All right.
But we don't tell Mom.

TRISTAN. Because I'm a rough time.

GUY. Yes.

(**GUY** *and* **TRISTAN** *do a special move that stands in for hugging.*)

Now go brush up.

(**TRISTAN** *drinks the espresso as they walk back inside.*)

(to us) Because when Tristan was around, these were the kind of words I heard. I'd come home and it wasn't –

(**FIONA** *appears. Lovingly...*)

FIONA. Love

GUY. Or –

FIONA. Loved

GUY. Or even –

FIONA. My baby!

GUY. It was –

(**FIONA** *confronts* **GUY** *in the living room.*)

FIONA. What in holy flipping hell did you give him?

GUY. Nothing.

FIONA. You did. You gave him a mid-life crisis.

(**TRISTAN** *crosses the room, still drinking the espresso. To no one in particular...*)

TRISTAN. I've wasted my life! I've gotten myself into something that I can never get out of!

GUY. I gave him a sip.

TRISTAN. *(offstage)* I'm having second thoughts!

FIONA. That's more than a sip.

      (**TRISTAN** *crosses the room again.*)

TRISTAN. I don't wanna live this shit life anymore! I'm such a fucking retard!

GUY. People say retard.

FIONA. Not in this house.

GUY. People say it all the time. And he wanted to know.

FIONA. I want to know string theory. I want to know the guitar. I want to know where you go at night. Doesn't mean I should.

GUY. Fiona, you need to stop being so, so –

      (**TRISTAN** *appears, holding a word.*)

TRISTAN. "Anal?"

GUY. Yes. No.

      (**TRISTAN** *digs into his pocket, tries another.*)

TRISTAN. "Oral?"

      (**GUY** *motions to* **TRISTAN**. *The universal kill gesture.*)

"Vaginal?" What. Daddy: what?

FIONA. Where did he get those?

      (**GUY** *shrugs.*)

Tris, show me what's in your pockets.

      (**TRISTAN** *keeps his hands in his pockets.*)

TRISTAN. What fucking asshat pockets?

      (**FIONA** *pulls* **TRISTAN**'s *hands out of his pockets.*)

GUY. Fiona –

TRISTAN. They're mine! I learned 'em! You can't!

FIONA. Yes, I can.

      (**TRISTAN** *struggles in* **FIONA**'s *grasp.*)

TRISTAN. Daddy's friend gave 'em to me!

FIONA. Did he now?

    *(**GUY** checks his cell phone.)*

GUY. I'm gonna take this call.

    *(**GUY** exits.)*

    Hey man, yeah –

TRISTAN. His phone didn't ring.

FIONA. Tristan.

    *(**FIONA** finds a jar and holds the open jar in front of **TRISTAN**. He doesn't move.)*

    You can't just repeat what other people say, okay? Especially Andy.

TRISTAN. Why?

FIONA. 'Cause Andy's been going through a lot lately and sometimes he says things he doesn't mean.

TRISTAN. Why?

FIONA. 'Cause Andy did a bad thing and so he's taking some time off work.

TRISTAN. He got fired?

FIONA. No. Just a leave,

    He's on a leave of absence, that's all.

TRISTAN. A what?

FIONA. A leave.

TRISTAN. A leaf?

FIONA. A leave.

TRISTAN. A tree?

FIONA. He's taking a break from work, that's all.

    Do you understand what that means?

TRISTAN. Yep.

FIONA. So why're we not listening to Andy?

TRISTAN. Because he's on a tree of absence.

    *(**FIONA** gives up. Good enough.)*

FIONA. Yes. He's on a tree of absence.

TRISTAN. But when does he get off?

FIONA. I don't know.

TRISTAN. *(beat)* What happened to our tree?

FIONA. Huh?

TRISTAN. In the backyard.

FIONA. We don't have a tree, honey.

TRISTAN. But we used to.

FIONA. No, we don't. We never have.

TRISTAN. At the old house?

FIONA. Tris, there is no old house. We've always lived here.

TRISTAN. You sure?

FIONA. Yeah. You probably just saw a picture, that's all. *(beat)* So can I get those from you?

> (**TRISTAN** *sadly looks at the words in his possession. Sigh. He hands over some of the words.* **FIONA** *places them inside the jar.*)

All of them.

TRISTAN. Can't I have just one?

FIONA. These're for grown-ups.

TRISTAN. Why?

FIONA. 'Cause grown-ups need them.

TRISTAN. Why?

FIONA. To cope.

TRISTAN. I cope.

FIONA. No, you don't.

TRISTAN. I do!

FIONA. Well, you shouldn't have to.
You use grown-up words, you have to know what they mean. Otherwise, you'll use them wrong and people will misunderstand you.

TRISTAN. Do people misunderstand you?

FIONA. All the time.

> (**TRISTAN** *places the rest of the words inside the jar.*)

FIONA. Thank you. And if you need to get something off your chest, you can tell me instead of the whole class.

TRISTAN. Why wouldn't I tell them?

FIONA. Because sometimes it's better to keep it a secret.

TRISTAN. Why would you keep a secret?

FIONA. Because –

> *(Lights up on* **GUY** *outside, now actually on the phone.* **TRISTAN** *and* **FIONA** *hear him for a moment.)*

GUY. – sometimes I don't know. I just don't see the point of it all, not even a little –

> *(Lights down on* **GUY**.*)*

FIONA. Now get in bed.

TRISTAN. *(relents)* All right.

> *(***TRISTAN** *turns to exit, then stops.)*

Do I still get to read the book tomorrow?

FIONA. Yes.

TRISTAN. In class?

FIONA. Yes.

TRISTAN. The whole way through?

FIONA. We'll see about that.

TRISTAN. I don't really think you stink. Not like a lot.

FIONA. Okay.

> *(***TRISTAN** *exits.* **GUY** *enters, still on the phone.)*

GUY. – yeah, no, shit move, totally.

> *(***FIONA** *thrusts the jar in front of* **GUY**.*)*

FIONA. You, too.

GUY. I'm on the fucking phone.

FIONA. Guy.

GUY. *(to phone)* Hold on a sec.

> *(***GUY** *opens his wallet, hands* **FIONA** *words. He digs into various pockets: breast pockets, back*

> *pockets, jacket pockets. He takes off his shoe, words*
> *pour out.* **GUY** *has a fucking huge vocabulary. A*
> *shitload.)*

FIONA. We need to talk.

GUY. I'm all outta words.

FIONA. Now.

GUY. *(to phone)* Call you back. Yeah. She's being a –

> *(**FIONA** holds up a word: "bitch.")*

FIONA. "Bitch?"

GUY. *(to phone)* I know, I know, it's retarded.

> *(**GUY** hangs up.)*

FIONA. What is wrong with you?

GUY. What can I say? Andy's got a foul mouth and kids love him.

You can't shield him.

FIONA. In this house, I can. There. See?

> *(**FIONA** screws a lid on the jar very tightly.)*

For when he's older.

GUY. So what're we supposed to say instead?

> *(**FIONA** hands him a set of words.)*

FIONA. Here.

> *(**GUY** flips through them.)*

GUY. This is fucking – *(as **FIONA** gives him the eye)* – fudging ridiculous.

FIONA. Like fudge it is.

GUY. This is hecka mentally challenged.

FIONA. Your friend is hecka mentally challenged.

GUY. I just don't see the point of it all.

FIONA. "Not even a little?"

GUY. Just because we don't say these things out loud doesn't make them not true. You can put it another way, but you can't put it away. You know there are things we can do.

FIONA. About what?

GUY. You mean about who. 'Cause Andy –

GUY/FIONA. " – had a girlfriend. Who had a kid."

FIONA. "She put him on drugs and it helped."

GUY. It did.

FIONA. Kids're meant to be a handful. He's fine.

GUY. But what about you, huh? What about you?

> (**FIONA** *hands* **GUY** *the jar to put away.* **GUY** *turns to us.*)

Fiona has a story. And it's been missing a lot lately.

> (*As if* **FIONA** *is speaking to reporters…*)

FIONA. We were driving

GUY. Home.

FIONA. I stop for

GUY. Gas.

FIONA. I go

GUY. Inside.

FIONA. And when I come back

GUY. No one.

FIONA. And when I get back

GUY. Nothing.

> (**GUY** *looks at the word jar. The words inside have disappeared. A convenient black hole.*)

Because Fiona has a story, and damned if I've heard it, from her at least. And life continues to be just another form of –

Scene

(Living room.)

(Back to the present. Where we were at the top of the previous scene.)

GUY. Difficult.

He was difficult, and there was nothing wrong with that. You know that, right?

(beat) So you ready now? We can still make it to dinner.

FIONA. Why is this so important?

GUY. Because that's what people do every couple of years? They eat? Like normal people.

FIONA. I eat.

GUY. At home. In the car. *(beat)* I thought we were going to talk about this. Twenty-four months, you said we'd talk about it. You said –

(The **DETECTIVE** *in the past appears.)*

DETECTIVE. Two years –

GUY. – right?

DETECTIVE. That's how long my last case took, Mrs. Hamlin. Started looking bleak, but two years and the parents finally got what was coming to them.

Sometimes that's how long it takes.

GUY. That's what you asked for.

FIONA. *(shrugs)* That's what he said.

DETECTIVE. On average.

Two years and maybe something good will grow.

(The **DETECTIVE** *disappears.)*

FIONA. In the time it takes for things to heal

For the sink to clog

The roof to leak

The paint to peel

And the dog to die,

In the time it takes for things to fall apart and for bad to get worse, that's how long we'll give it.

GUY. So two.

FIONA. Yeah.

GUY. *(question)* Two years and we'll go out and we'll make ourselves better.

FIONA. I guess. I hope.

>   *(Return to the present...)*

GUY. That's what you told me at the time.
   You said twenty-four months and we'd move on.

FIONA. Just because you say something doesn't make it true.

GUY. *(question)* Really.

FIONA. Yeah.

GUY. Well, love you, too.

FIONA. And twenty-four months is nothing, if you think about it.

GUY. Really? 'Cause I remember when twenty-four months was basically forever to you. 'Cause when we first got Tristan, I said twenty-four months old and you said –

>   *(Back to* GUY *and* FIONA *in the past, much earlier.)*

FIONA. That long?

GUY. You said –

FIONA. That old?

GUY. So what? He's twenty-four months, he's healthy, he's happy, he's –

>   *(*GUY *hands* FIONA *a photograph.)*

   – here. Ta da!

FIONA. And what does that have to do with us?

GUY. Andy knows this girl. Who had a kid.

FIONA. And what?

GUY. And now she's wondering whether we might want to make him ours.

FIONA. Why us?

GUY. She heard we'd been trying to have a kid.

> She heard we'd been trying for a while.

> And that you were a teacher and we were a couple.

FIONA. Guy.

GUY. She's a kid who had a kid.

> And now she's trying to figure out what to do with him.

FIONA. So...?

GUY. So she was wondering –

FIONA. No.

GUY. Hear me out.

FIONA. I did!

GUY. We've always wanted a kid. We've been trying to have a kid.

FIONA. We said a kid, we meant a baby.

GUY. We may not get another chance like this. If not now, then when?

FIONA. When we're older.

GUY. We're older.

FIONA. Uh huh.

GUY. And older.

FIONA. Guy –

GUY. We're older than we've ever been.

FIONA. Hah.

GUY. Just meet him.

FIONA. And?

GUY. And see him.

FIONA. And then?

GUY. And if he's not for us, he can just be somebody else's problem. *(beat)* She won't even be there.

FIONA. Oh.

GUY. Okay?

FIONA. Okay.

*(Fast-forward to **GUY** and **FIONA** meeting the toddler **TRISTAN** for the first time. They lean into the crib.)*

FIONA. He's small.

GUY. He's sleeping.

FIONA. He's perfect.

GUY. He's ours.

FIONA. He's talking, he's walking.

GUY. He's running, he's reading.

FIONA. He's everything you said he'd be.

GUY. He's wandering

He's wondering

He's asking where he comes from –

FIONA. And what did you say?

GUY. Where does anyone come from?

The stork. I said a stork and a tree and a bundle of joy.

(beat) You could tell him.

FIONA. *I* could tell him?

GUY. You have a way of putting things.

FIONA. *("no")* Guy.

GUY. *(shrugs)* He wants to know where people come from.

FIONA. People come from people. He comes from us. And that's enough.

GUY. 'Cause you know, this came in the mail.

*(**GUY** drops off a letter: a pink piece of paper and matching envelope.)*

FIONA. A letter?

GUY. For Tris. From his mother. *(corrects)* His birth mother.

*(**FIONA** places the unopened pink letter in her jar.)*

FIONA. I'll save it. For later. When he's better. When he'll understand.

GUY. When is that?

FIONA. Your guess is as good as mine.

GUY. But what should I tell her?

FIONA. The woman?

GUY. The mom.

FIONA. "Take care of your things. We do."

> *(This is kind of harsh. GUY's face registers this.)*

Or nothing. Tell her nothing.

GUY. What about him? *(beat)* We could tell him. You don't think he already kind of suspects?

FIONA. No. He's fine.

> *(FIONA puts the jar with the pink letter up on a shelf.)*

GUY. He is?

FIONA. He's ADHD.

GUY. He's something.

FIONA. He'll grow out of it.

He's three.

GUY. He's four.

FIONA. He's pre-K.

He's okay.

GUY. He's up and he's down.

He's kicking and screaming.

He's all over the place.

FIONA. So was I when I was five and a half.

Six and three quarters.

Seven and a day.

He's what he's always been: a walking, talking encyclopedia.

He's –

> *(TED appears. In conversation with FIONA.)*

TED. – difficult.

FIONA. What?

TED. He's been difficult.

FIONA. Ted: in what way?

TED. In every way.

FIONA. *(to* **GUY***)* First week, second grade, Tris is just getting used to the schedule and Ted, the new principal, comes up to me and says –

TED. – difficult. Richard tells me he's been difficult in class.

FIONA. In terms of what?

TED. Tristan said when he grows up, he wants to be a tree.

GUY. A tree?

FIONA. I know!

GUY. What's wrong with that?

FIONA. That's what I said!

GUY. A tree is good.

    A tree is grounded.

    A tree shows he has imagination.

FIONA. Exactly!

TED. Richard tells me: one minute he's fine and the next – !

    It's like night and day

    Black and white

    Brown and sticky.

FIONA. What?

TED. You know what I mean.

FIONA. He's seven and seven-year-olds flip out sometimes.

    Just give him his book,

    Let him go outside,

    And I bet you he'll be fine.

TED. This is second grade, Fiona. It doesn't work like that anymore.

FIONA. He can recite that nature book of his cover to cover, back to front.

TED. And that doesn't concern you?

FIONA. Ted: if he's difficult, he's bored.

TED. Or he might fit in better in Joanne's class.

FIONA. What?

GUY. What?

(**TED** *disappears.*)

FIONA. I had to.

GUY. You put him in your class?

FIONA. I had no other choice. Where else could we put him?

GUY. Joanne's class?

FIONA. That's not a choice. That's a death sentence.
    That's district money for every kid they put in that special ed class.

GUY. But if he needs it?

FIONA. He needs her class like he needs a hole in his head.

GUY. Like he needs a mouth to breathe?

FIONA. Guy.

GUY. It's just second grade.

FIONA. And the beginning of the rest of his life.

GUY. So a month?

FIONA. Or two. He'll be in my class,
    He'll be under my watch,
    He'll get what he needs,
    Which is just more outside time.
    And in two months, Ted'll make the call.

GUY. You sure?

FIONA. We'll take it day by day by day –

        (*Time passes.*)

    – after day after day after day after –

GUY. Dinner?

FIONA. What?

GUY. After dinner, after we tuck him in, you want to talk?

FIONA. Why?

GUY. Just a word.

FIONA. I'm fine.
    I'm thin.
    I'm spare.
    I'm spent.

GUY. Well, you look exhausted.

FIONA. I'm just a little easy on the eyes, that's all.

GUY. What happened?

FIONA. He got into my dirty laundry and he found this.

(**FIONA** *holds up the photograph.*)

GUY. A picture?

FIONA. The picture.

GUY. Of him and the birth mother?

FIONA. Yes.

GUY. He knew it was him?

FIONA. He's seven,

He's smart:

So yes.

GUY. What did you tell him?

FIONA. I said she was a friend of a friend,

Someone that he used to know.

GUY. But don't you think we should tell him?

FIONA. Sure. Soon.

GUY. When is that?

FIONA. When he's in a place to hear it.

GUY. And where is he now?

FIONA. In the backyard.

GUY. It's getting dark.

FIONA. Give him another minute. In fact, give me one, too.

(**FIONA** *sits down, exhausted.*)

GUY. Whatever happened to us, huh?

FIONA. We wanted a kid and we got Tristan.

GUY. We got our son and lost ourselves.

FIONA. He's what we signed up for.

GUY. Let's go.

FIONA. Where?

GUY. Somewhere. Anywhere.
    We'll sneak out the front.
    We'll get in the car.
    And it'll be like we were never here at all.
    Let's go.

FIONA. Just the two of us?

GUY. Let's go now.

FIONA. Stop saying that.

GUY. I'm just saying: a break. We could really use a break.

FIONA. Soon.

GUY. Tomorrow?

FIONA. Tomorrow's Picture Day.

GUY. Tomorrow's your birthday.

FIONA. So let me get through tomorrow, let me get a little
    bit older, a little bit wiser, and then it'll all be better.

GUY. You sure?

FIONA. Tomorrow, he'll take his picture, read his book –

GUY. Again?

FIONA. Every Friday, that's what I promised him.

GUY. The same book?

FIONA. He enjoys it.

GUY. And the other kids?

FIONA. Doesn't matter. All they have to do is sit there and
    listen.

            (GUY *turns to exit.*)

    Tristan's old house.

GUY. Yeah?

FIONA. Did it have a tree? In the backyard?

GUY. Maybe. Why?

FIONA. No reason.

            (GUY *exits.* FIONA *examines the word jar. She
            stares at the pink letter inside. She unscrews the
            lid a bit. A woman's voice, whispered words spill
            out – .*)

VOICE. To my baby
   Hope you
   Miss you
   Miss me
   And get what's
   Coming to you
   From me

> (**FIONA** *screws the lid back on, tight, and waits.*)

FIONA. *(to herself)* For later.

> (**TRISTAN** *enters with his green and blue sweater stuck over his head.*)

TRISTAN. Help me.

> (**TRISTAN** *flaps his sleeves helplessly. It's charming.*)

Mom: help me.

FIONA. You want me to help?

> (**TRISTAN** *nods.*)

And you won't scream?

> (**TRISTAN** *shakes his head.*)

Okaaaay.

> (**FIONA** *helps* **TRISTAN** *get his sweater off. Then she throws her arms around him. Big hug.* **TRISTAN** *groans, slightly disgruntled.*)

Can I hold you?
Can I just hold you?
I used to.
I used to and you liked it.
What happened to that, huh?
What happened to that?

> (**TRISTAN** *tries to wriggle from her grasp, but she holds tighter. She closes her eyes, she smells him.*)

(**TRISTAN** *wriggles out of her grasp and disappears.*
FIONA *doesn't seem to notice. She's left holding the*
sweater.)

FIONA. *(to us)* That's what I remember.

And if that's difficult, well, I didn't see it.

Scene

(Living room.)

(Back to the present. **GUY** *with the home phone.)*

GUY. We got a call.

FIONA. From the restaurant? About dinner?

GUY. No. From the school.

FIONA. From Ted?

GUY. I would assume so.

FIONA. I'll listen to it later.

GUY. You're not curious?

FIONA. No.

GUY. I bet he wants to give you your job back.

FIONA. I have a job.

GUY. Looking is not a job.

Looking for someone is not something to spend all your time on.

FIONA. Well, it's what I spend my time on.

Ted made it pretty clear when he fired me –

GUY. It was a leave of absence. And if he's calling now –

FIONA. It's been two years.

GUY. Exactly.

FIONA. No.

GUY. It was one day.

It was one bad day.

Picture Day's always bad, right?

So just call him.

Just call him and say –

FIONA. What? "Hey, Ted?"

(The **PRINCIPAL** *appears, at the start of a conversation.)*

PRINCIPAL. Fiona.

(Camera flash. We go back into the past.)

Scene

(Picture Day.)

*(**FIONA** about to leave the school. She cleans off her hands. Ted the **PRINCIPAL** corners her.)*

PRINCIPAL. A word?

FIONA. Which word?

PRINCIPAL. Tristan. It's about Tristan.

FIONA. *(joke)* Little more than a word there.

PRINCIPAL. So more than a word. Several words.

FIONA. Can this wait? I got Tristan in the car.

PRINCIPAL. And how's he doing?

FIONA. Why?

PRINCIPAL. Is he okay?

FIONA. Why wouldn't he be?

PRINCIPAL. Kayla's mother is here now and –

FIONA. You know, Ted, really, can we talk tomorrow?

*(**FIONA** edges towards the door.)*

PRINCIPAL. We're gonna go ahead and switch his class.

*(**FIONA** stops.)*

FIONA. Ted, we agreed –

PRINCIPAL. You said two months: we've given you three. It was against policy to even let him be in your class in the first place. Joanne'll take him, and maybe a special class, more one-on-one education'll solve the problem –

FIONA. Children like him don't need more attention.

PRINCIPAL. You sure about that?

FIONA. And if you want a retard, Joanne's the retard.

PRINCIPAL. Fiona.

FIONA. You move him, I'll transfer him.
    You move him, I'll quit.

PRINCIPAL. About that. About what's been happening in
   your class.

FIONA. Yes?

PRINCIPAL. Here.

> *(The* **PRINCIPAL** *hands a folded paper to* **FIONA**.*)*

FIONA. A letter?

PRINCIPAL. A leave.

FIONA. *(question)* A leaf.

PRINCIPAL. *(slowly)* A leave. A leave of absence.

FIONA. *(tries to understand)* A leeeeeafff of absence.

PRINCIPAL. *(together)* A leeeeeeeeeavvvvvve of absence.

FIONA. *(together)* A leeeeeeeeeafffffff of absence.

> *(The* **PRINCIPAL** *then takes out the leave of
> absence, which is actually a small tree of absence.)*

A treeeeeee of absence?

PRINCIPAL. Just for now.

   Think of this as an opportunity.

   Take some time, and you can come right back to where
   you leafed off.

FIONA. Left off?

PRINCIPAL. Fiona, please.

FIONA. C'mon, Ted. It's always crazy on Picture Day, you
   know that.

PRINCIPAL. You've been distracted, we've had complaints –

FIONA. About what?

PRINCIPAL. I think you know.

> *(The* **PRINCIPAL** *produces* **FIONA**'*s dirty laundry.)*

FIONA. Where did you get that?

PRINCIPAL. Facts're facts and socks're socks.

> *(The* **PRINCIPAL** *pulls out* **FIONA**'*s socks, shirts,
> underwear. It's incriminating evidence.)*

FIONA. Ted, I didn't –

   We don't.

PRINCIPAL. Me? I don't care what you do, but air your dirty
laundry out at home, okay?

> (**FIONA** *grabs the dirty laundry from the*
> **PRINCIPAL**.)

FIONA. Seriously, can we talk about this?

PRINCIPAL. We have.

Tristan can go to Joanne and you can take a break –

FIONA. Ted, do I look like I need a break?

PRINCIPAL. It's just a tree.

Don't make this bigger than it is, okay?

FIONA. How long?

PRINCIPAL. Six months.

Foot and a half.

Take it home, give it some water

And maybe something good'll grow.

I'll leaf it right here.

This is nothing against you.

You're great with kids. Just not your kid.

FIONA. Happy Picture Day, Ted.

> (**FIONA** *exits with her tree of absence and her dirty*
> *laundry.*)

Scene

(In the car.)

(**FIONA** *gets into the car with her tree of absence, dirty laundry, etc.)*

(**TRISTAN** *is already in the car, fidgeting.)*

FIONA. Let's go home, Tris.

TRISTAN. *(re: tree)* What's that?

FIONA. It's a leave of absence.

TRISTAN. Looks like a tree.

FIONA. *("fine")* Yes. It's a tree. It's a tree of absence.

TRISTAN. I want a tree of absence.

FIONA. Well, it's only for me.

TRISTAN. Why?

FIONA. Because it's a lovely parting gift.

TRISTAN. I want a lovely parting gift.

FIONA. You have to be leaving first, in order to part.

TRISTAN. Are you leaving?

FIONA. Yes, I'm leaving.

TRISTAN. For where?

FIONA. Home. We're leaving for home.

TRISTAN. 'Cause I stink.

FIONA. Yes.

(**TRISTAN** *fidgets.)*

Now stop picking at it.

(**TRISTAN** *tries to stay still.)*

Next week, we're going to move you over to Mrs. Hoffstadt's class, okay?

TRISTAN. Why?

FIONA. Because you need help.
Sometimes people need a little extra help, even if they don't say so, okay?

TRISTAN. Okay.

FIONA. Truce?

TRISTAN. What's a truce?

FIONA. It means we agree to let bygones be bygones, Tristans be Tristans.

It means we agree to call a spade a spade.

TRISTAN. What's a spade?

FIONA. A shovel. It's something you use to bury yourself in shit with. *(corrects)* Shoot with.

TRISTAN. What does that mean?

FIONA. It means you're my baby. And you always will be.

TRISTAN. Always?

FIONA. Yep.

TRISTAN. When I'm eight?

FIONA. Yep.

TRISTAN. When I'm nine?

FIONA. Even then.

TRISTAN. But I'll be dead by then.

FIONA. What?

TRISTAN. When I'm ten?

When I'm eleven?

FIONA. Even when you're out of sight and out of mind, you'll never be out of my hair.

TRISTAN. And that's a good thing?

FIONA. Sometimes.

>   (FIONA *offers her non-driving hand.*)

Hug?

>   (FIONA *and* TRISTAN *link fingers. The hug stand-in.*)

Now sit still.

>   (*As* FIONA *drives,* TRISTAN *disappears.*)

>   (FIONA *doesn't notice at first, but then she sees the empty seat. Camera flash.*)

Scene

(Living room.)

(Back to the present.)

GUY. And that's it?

FIONA. Yes.

GUY. *(question)* Really.

FIONA. There's nothing after that because he was gone after that.

GUY. And?

FIONA. And honestly, I don't want to talk about it.

GUY. With me. You don't want to talk about it with me.

FIONA. You know what happened:

(The **MAN** *crosses the stage.)*

MAN. "We were driving home.

I stop for gas.

I go inside.

And when I come back, no one.

And when I get back, nothing."

GUY. Sure. From the newspaper, the police, the mailman. But how about I hear it from you?

(beat) Do you remember what you said to me, that day?

FIONA. No, honestly.

GUY. Nothing?

FIONA. If there's something other than nothing, I don't remember.

GUY. Really.

FIONA. If I said something, tell me what I said then. What did I say that was so important?

GUY. Nothing.

FIONA. See?

GUY. You said nothing.

You came home and you said –

*(Flashback to **FIONA** and **GUY** in the living room.)*

*(**GUY** sits on the couch, waiting. **FIONA** enters with her tree of absence. She takes a couple steps forward and opens her mouth. Nothing comes out. She sits down on the couch, though slightly too far apart from **GUY**.)*

(A chasm builds between them. A moment, then...)

FIONA. Nothing.

GUY. Nothing?

FIONA. That's what they said.

They said they'll call us if there's anything.

But for now: now we do nothing.

GUY. Okay.

FIONA. I called you.

GUY. Hm?

FIONA. Earlier.

GUY. I guess I didn't see.

FIONA. Oh.

GUY. But there's something you want to tell me, though, right?

FIONA. Tell you later

(Time begins to pass.)

And later

And later

And later –

(The seasons change.)

GUY. So when?

FIONA. When I'm ready

When I'm older

When he's older than he'll ever be, ever been

When he's a second thought

When it's not a rough time for me.

GUY. So when?

FIONA. So never.

Is never okay?

GUY. You coming to bed at least?

FIONA. I will.

When the cows come home.

When pigs fly.

Once in a blue moon.

GUY. So soon.

FIONA. Yeah, soon.

GUY. I'll see you then.

FIONA. Okay.

> (**GUY** *picks up the tree of absence.*)

GUY. What do you want to do with this?

FIONA. Put it in back. I'll deal with it later.

GUY. Good night.

FIONA. I'll try to.

> (**GUY** *places the tree of absence outside.*)

GUY. *(in the present)* You came home and you had words for everyone else but me. You came home and you couldn't even tell me –

> (**FIONA** *enters from a long day of talking to other people. She tosses her empty word jar on the couch.*)

GUY. How was it?

Fiona?

Police say anything new?

> (**FIONA** *sighs.* **GUY** *holds up an envelope of Picture Day photos.*)

GUY. The school sent the pictures. From Picture Day. You want to open it?

> (**FIONA** *shrugs and perches herself somewhere.*)

GUY. You okay?

> (**FIONA** *gestures to her empty word jar.*)

GUY. Oh. Tomorrow?

    *(**FIONA** shrugs.)*

GUY. Okay. We'll talk tomorrow.

    (Back to the present.)

And tomorrow and tomorrow and tomorrow –

Can we make tomorrow today?

Just for today, can today be tomorrow?

FIONA. Why?

GUY. Because it's time.

Because there's no gift like the present.

Because I can't make it better if you don't tell me how.

Fiona?

FIONA. In a minute.

GUY. Okay. When you want to talk, let me know.

    *(**GUY** turns for the front door.)*

FIONA. Where're you going?

GUY. Nowhere. We're going nowhere, right?

FIONA. Guy.

    *(**FIONA** goes to the threshold of the front door. She looks forwards towards **GUY**, already going off into the night. Then a noise from outside.)*

Tris?

    *(**FIONA** looks around. Outside, in the backyard, a motion-sensor light switches on. **FIONA** looks back towards the yard. But there's nothing.)*

Scene

(A bar.)

ANDY. So what happened?

GUY. What.

ANDY. You're here with me. Now. So what happened?

GUY. Eh.

ANDY. Don't want to talk about it?

GUY. Nothing to talk about, Andy. Not with her, anyway.

ANDY. Still?

GUY. Yeah.

ANDY. Twenty-four months and she can't even make it to dinner?

GUY. I tried.

ANDY. Shit, 'cause two years's a long time to go without eating out once in a while, if you know what I'm saying!

GUY. I do.

ANDY. You give her the cupcake for me?

GUY. Yeah.

ANDY. And?

GUY. Nothing.

ANDY. Well! It's her party, she can cry if she wants to.

GUY. But that's just the thing.

She doesn't.

She won't. Not with me anyway.

And the funny thing is –

ANDY. Yeah?

GUY. I don't know. I just don't know.

ANDY. And you can't expect to.

Shit: you've been through a fucking rough fucking time.

Your kid's gone, been two years: rough fucking fucking time.

GUY. To her, I'm just something to fall back on.

ANDY. So you're a mattress.

    She thinks you're her fucking fucking mattress.

GUY. Yeah!

ANDY. A big softie.

GUY. I know!

ANDY. I had a girl and a futon like that.

    It's nice for a while, but no way to fucking fuck.

GUY. Right?!

ANDY. 'Cause: you?

    You're a Guy.

GUY. Yeah –

ANDY. You're a guy's guy!

GUY. I am!

ANDY. You're your own man!

GUY. That's right, huh?!

ANDY. And asking her to

    Get out

    Get up

    Get off

    Once in a while?

    That's not too much to ask for, is it?

GUY. Is it?

ANDY. Is it!

GUY. It isn't!

ANDY. No!

GUY. Yeah – ! Or no!

ANDY. She still on that tree of absence?

GUY. Yep. And it's a real weeping willow.

ANDY. That bad, huh?

GUY. Yep.

ANDY. Ah, jeez.

    How long's that shit been?

        *(**GUY** gestures "this long.")*

ANDY. That tall, huh?

GUY. It was only supposed to last six months and now, two years and a foot and a half later?

ANDY. What she needs:

She needs to get herself off.

GUY. How?

ANDY. You get off by letting yourself off.

You get down by going through,

If you know what I mean.

GUY. I think I know what you mean.

>   (**ANDY** *gives* **GUY** *a look.*)

No, I know what you mean!

ANDY. You know what I'm saying!

GUY. I do!

ANDY. You don't cut that shit down:

You're gonna wake up to a fucking tree of abstinence.

GUY. Already have.

ANDY. Oohf: that's rough.

'Cause you may not have answers, but you always got needs.

GUY. Tell me about it.

ANDY. Say, you call my girl yet?

GUY. I did.

ANDY. And?

GUY. And I didn't.

ANDY. What do you mean?

GUY. I called her up, I heard her voice, and it was like I was talking to my wife all over again.

>   (*Flashback to* **GUY** *holds up a business card with a number scrawled on the back. He's on the phone.* **FIONA** *answers the other end.*)

FIONA. Hello?

GUY. My friend Andy gave me your number?

FIONA. *(suspicious)* What?

GUY. I thought maybe you could tell me what you're wearing...? If that's okay?

FIONA. Who is this?!

GUY. Fiona?

FIONA. Who are you? Really.

GUY. I don't know.

FIONA. And does your wife know?

GUY. I don't think she does either. But she used to.

FIONA. I used to, too, know someone like you.

GUY. And where's that someone now?

FIONA. Where he always is. Out. *(beat)* What do you want from me?

GUY. What my wife won't tell me.

FIONA. That you suck?

That you blow?

GUY. That I've been a bad guy lately.

FIONA. That I love you?

That I hate you?

That I need you like I need a hole in my head?

Like I need a mouth to breathe?

That I don't think we love each other. Not even a little?

GUY. I'm just looking for a date.

FIONA. You mean a fuck.

GUY. An end.

A time when this is all over.

I need to know that there's a light at the end of the tunnel.

That there's an end to the tunnel.

If not twenty-four months, then when?

FIONA. I don't know if I can give you that.

GUY. Why not?

FIONA. I should go. I should leave.

GUY. Can I call you again?

FIONA. I don't think my husband would like that. We have a kid.

GUY. We *had* a kid.

FIONA. Well, *I* have a kid. He's coming home soon. And I don't want to miss him, even if I do.

(**FIONA** *hangs up, quietly.* **ANDY** *looks at* **GUY**.)

GUY. *(shrugs)* I called. She had to go.

ANDY. Try her later.

(**GUY** *hands the business card back to* **ANDY**.)

GUY. I think I'm good.

ANDY. Well, lemme know! Sooner or later, one of you's got to do something. You can't live like that forever!

GUY. Whatever happened to her?

ANDY. Who?

GUY. Tristan's mother? His birth mother.

ANDY. Oh, her? She shot herself.

(*Following is in constant rewind…*)

GUY. She what?

ANDY. She joined the army.

GUY. She what?

ANDY. She got her GED.

GUY. She what?

ANDY. She flew the coop.
    She popped the weasel.
    She put the bomp in the bompbahbompbah.
    She put the ram in the ramalamadingdong.
    She kicked the bucket and then the tires.
    She did everything.
    (fondly) Boy, oh boy, did she do everything.
    But I'll tell you, [the] one thing she never did?

GUY. Yeah?

ANDY. Never got over.

GUY. What do you mean?

ANDY. She killed herself.

GUY. Why?

ANDY. She was a kid. Who had a kid. You do the math.
  She couldn't handle things and she went under.

GUY. You never told me that.

ANDY. You know she died.

GUY. I never knew it happened like that.

ANDY. I figured it was obvious.

GUY. What happened to the dad?

ANDY. Stories like that, there's never a dad.
  Just a name on the paper.
  Just a guy who used to live with her, that's all.

    (Pause.)

GUY. I should go. I should leave.

ANDY. Listen, I know what you're going through.

GUY. I don't think you do.

    (**ANDY** *offers another business card.*)

ANDY. Fine, but I got a guy. Who's got a practice.

GUY. *(reads)* "Family law."

ANDY. Two years, your kid's gone,
  Your life's shit and cupcake?
  I'm just saying –

GUY. We have a kid.

ANDY. You *had* a kid. And you know that's not the same.

GUY. I should go. I should leave.

ANDY. Leave what?
  Leave me?
  Leave here?
  Leave her?

GUY. I should go. That's all. I should just go.

ANDY. And yet, you don't. Why is that?

GUY. I don't know what you're talking about.

ANDY. You know:

    I once had an idea of a person I wanted to be when I grew up. And –

GUY. And?

ANDY. Think he became you. Nice guy, that guy.

    I should dig him up.

    He's been buried in shit for a while.

    I should dig him up and give him a call.

    Nice guy, that you.

    But if you see him, tell him I want him back, okay?

    'Cause he's not the guy you used to be.

GUY. That guy wasn't so good either.

ANDY. Well, at least he wouldn't have let other people go through things for him.

GUY. I don't do that.

ANDY. Oh come on, we all know:

    You let her go through that shit so you won't have to.

GUY. You know: I once had a friend who gave a shit.

    He helped. And it helped.

ANDY. Figured that was what I've been doing all along.

GUY. Just gimme your keys. I'll get it out of the trunk now.

ANDY. What?

GUY. The box.

ANDY. The which box?

GUY. The white box.

ANDY. The toys? Dropped it off. Like you said.

GUY. No, I didn't.

ANDY. Think you did.

GUY. I said take it off my hands for me.

ANDY. And I did. To Goodwill.

GUY. What did you do that for?!

ANDY. You said you were done with her shit.

    You said you were serious this time.

    So I thought you were.

GUY. All our photos were in there!

ANDY. How was I supposed to know?

GUY. Where did you take it?

ANDY. You're not going to find it. It's too late.

GUY. *Where is it?*

ANDY. *(beat)* It's the one on Pine and Spruce.

> (**ANDY** *holds up another business card.*)

You can try, but you're not gonna find what you're looking for. You know that, right?

> (**GUY** *takes the card, runs off.*)

Scene

> *(Living room.)*

> *(**FIONA** on her phone listening to her voicemail messages.)*

GUY'S VOICE. Hey, Fiona, we're almost home.
We just ran into some traffic.
He had to go.
Tris, say hi.

TRISTAN'S VOICE. Hi.

GUY'S VOICE. Hi who?

TRISTAN'S VOICE. Hi, Mom.

> *(**FIONA** repeats the message, over and over.)*

Hi, Mom
Hi, Mom
Mom
Mom

> *(The door swings open. The **DETECTIVE** stands in the threshold. She doesn't recognize him at first.)*

DETECTIVE. Mom?
Mom?

> *(**FIONA** just stares at the **DETECTIVE**.)*

Ma'am?
Ma'am?

FIONA. *(recognizes)* Detective?

DETECTIVE. Mrs. Hamlin.

FIONA. Sorry, I just thought you were someone else.

DETECTIVE. I get that a lot. I just have one of those faces!
(beat) Bad time?

FIONA. *(a joke)* When is it ever good!

> *(The **DETECTIVE** takes out a folder.)*

DETECTIVE. I brought you something.

FIONA. A folder?

DETECTIVE. The case.

FIONA. The what?

DETECTIVE. Two years. We're closing the case. *(re: folder)* So, I figured you'd want your things back.

FIONA. But I just spoke with you! I gave you evidence! I gave you cantaloupe!

DETECTIVE. Technically, you gave me hives.

FIONA. Wait, you can't do this. Not until we know what happened.

DETECTIVE. It's been two years: I think we all know what happened.

(**FIONA** *blocks the* **DETECTIVE***'s path.*)

Mrs. Hamlin? I have to go.

FIONA. Please. Stay. I appreciate you coming by. *(re: folder)* Dropping this off.

DETECTIVE. I was on my way to see my mom anyway.

FIONA. She lives around here?

DETECTIVE. She used to.

FIONA. Oh.

DETECTIVE. It was a long time ago.

FIONA. Do you have any more questions for me at least?

DETECTIVE. Mrs. Hamlin, we've gone over this before.

FIONA. If you're going to close it, I just want to know you're being thorough, that's all.

DETECTIVE. Okay.

(*The* **DETECTIVE** *takes out a notebook. From a routine missing persons questionnaire…*)

On the day of the disappearance, what was he wearing?

FIONA. A sweater. A green and blue sweater.

DETECTIVE. And his shoe size?

FIONA. He wears a two.

DETECTIVE. Now.

FIONA. What?

DETECTIVE. What is his shoe size *now*?

FIONA. I don't know.

DETECTIVE. If he grows at a rate of three inches per year and eight pounds per season and a train leaves Philadelphia traveling sixty miles an hour at four in the morning, how tall is he now?

FIONA. I'm not sure.

DETECTIVE. At the time of his disappearance, did you love him?

Did you need him?

Did you leave him?

If he came through that door, sat on your couch, took out his notebook, and asked you this question, what would you say to him?

> *(***FIONA*** *looks at the* ***DETECTIVE*** *and sees* ***TRISTAN*** *in him.)*

FIONA. I've missed you.

DETECTIVE. Uh huh.

FIONA. And I'm sorry.

DETECTIVE. Okay.

FIONA. And I'm glad that you're back.

> *(The* ***DETECTIVE*** *unbuttons his jacket. The green and blue sweater underneath.)*

DETECTIVE. Did you know her?

Did you see her?

Did you meet her?

Did you try to?

FIONA. No.

No.

No.

Once.

DETECTIVE. And?

FIONA. And she died.

And the problem went away.

And I was happy for a while.

DETECTIVE. Am I good?

    Am I gone?

    Am I gay?

    Am I straight?

    Was I married?

    Was I separated?

    Was I drowned?

    Was I dredged?

    Was I strangled?

    Was I worth it?

FIONA. I don't know

    I don't know

    I don't know

    I don't know

    I don't know

    I don't know

    I don't know

    I don't know

    I don't know

    Yes.

DETECTIVE. And what would you do to get me back?

FIONA. Anything.

DETECTIVE. Then why didn't you? *(back to normal)* But Mrs. Hamlin, unless there's anything else I should know about, I should get going.

FIONA. So what happened to her?

DETECTIVE. Who?

FIONA. Your mom.

DETECTIVE. Oh, she died.

FIONA. How?

DETECTIVE. She was by herself.

    She was late at night.

    She was two months off her meds, three months overdue for a checkup.

She went in back.

She got some rope.

She made a swing.

FIONA. And?

DETECTIVE. She swung.

FIONA. Wait, Tristan –

DETECTIVE. I should get going. It's past my bedtime. My mom's gonna be mad.

FIONA. I'm not. It's okay –

DETECTIVE. Mrs. Hamlin, I have to go.

> (**FIONA** *reaches for the* **DETECTIVE**. *As he squirms more, he becomes* **TRISTAN**.)

I have to go!

> (*The* **DETECTIVE** *– now* **TRISTAN** *– slips out the back into the yard.*)

FIONA. TRISTAN!

> (**FIONA** *follows. She swings the back doors open.*)

> (*In front of her, suddenly, inexplicably, is a massive tree. Or maybe just the shadow of one. Perhaps this is the magnified shadow of* **FIONA**'s *tiny leave/tree of absence.*)

TRISTAN!

TRISTAN!

> (*From behind* **FIONA**, *in the threshold, another shadow materializes: a figure appears.*)

> (**FIONA** *turns. It's* **GUY**. *He holds the white box.*)

GUY. Fiona.

FIONA. Guy.

> (**GUY** *looks up at the tree.*)

FIONA. You see it, too?

GUY. The tree?

FIONA. Yeah.

GUY. All the time.

FIONA. Me, too.

GUY. I need to show you something.

> (**FIONA** *finally notices the white box that* **GUY** *holds.*)

FIONA. You found the box.

GUY. Yeah.

FIONA. You found the pictures.

GUY. No.

FIONA. What?

> (**GUY** *opens the box. It's empty.*)

GUY. I just thought if I took it away, you'd get better.
  If I took it away, you'd stop thinking about it.

FIONA. You were the one who took them. You took the photos.

GUY. I just thought, out of sight, out of mind.

> (**GUY** *drops the empty box on the floor.*)

But I went to Goodwill and they'd lost them.
(corrects) I'd lost them.
Our pictures.
I'm so sorry.
I just wish we could be the kind of people who could have a happy birthday, who tell each other things in plain English.

FIONA. Me, too.

GUY. So can we?

> (**FIONA** *looks up from the empty box.*)

FIONA. I don't think you'd understand.

GUY. Why not?

FIONA. That day, I came home and you said –

GUY. "Nothing?"

FIONA. You said –

GUY. "Okay."

　　I said –

FIONA. "But there's something you want to tell me, though, right?"

GUY. That's not what I meant.

FIONA. But that's what I heard.

　　I came home and I could read it all over your face,

　　Like I got what I always had coming.

　　Like there was something else I could've done.

GUY. And you don't think I feel like that, too?

FIONA. You weren't even there.

GUY. I know.

FIONA. You weren't even close.

GUY. But you called.

FIONA. Yes?

GUY. You called for me to come and pick up Tris.

　　　　(Flashback to a phone ringing. And ringing. And then –)

FIONA. I called and you were

　　　　*(**GUY** answers as his voicemail.)*

GUY. Busy.

FIONA. You were

GUY. Out.

FIONA. You were

GUY. Not here right now.

FIONA. You were

　　　　*(Flashback to **GUY**'s voicemail on Picture Day.)*

GUY. Sorry

　　I'm not here right now.

　　Sorry I'm not here for you right now.

　　Sorry I'm not in three places at once.

　　Sorry I'm not everything

　　Everywhere

GUY. *(cont.)* Every man
    You want me to be.
    Sorry I'm not
    Braver
    Stronger
    Faster
    Smarter
    You.
    Sorry I'm not and never have been.
    But if you'd've left a message,
    Called me except to yell at me,
    Taken a break for once,
    Been the kind of person I once fell in love with –
    But if you leave a message
    If you leaf a message, I'll try to be next time.

       (Beep.)

FIONA. I called and you weren't there.
    So it's no one's fault but mine.

GUY. That's not true.

FIONA. Isn't it?

GUY. Fiona, that day, you called and I was with a client.

FIONA. I know.

GUY. I saw you were calling –

       *(The **MAN** as a **CLIENT**.)*

CLIENT. And?

GUY. Nothing.

CLIENT. And?

GUY. No one.

CLIENT. You sure?

GUY. Just my wife.

       *(**GUY** puts away his phone.)*

GUY. *(back to present)* I saw that you called, and I did nothing.

And to me, that's just as bad,

Probably worse.

FIONA. Oh.

GUY. So can you tell me then?

FIONA. What.

GUY. Whatever it is you wanted to say, when you called.

FIONA. What was there to say? It was an ordinary day.

MAN. Wrong.

FIONA. It was Picture Day.

MAN. Yes.

FIONA. And it was his day to read to the class, after lunch.

MAN. And?

FIONA. And he wasn't feeling well.

MAN. Wrong.

FIONA. And he was a little restless.

MAN. Wrong.

FIONA. And he had tantrum written all over him.

> *(The* **MAN** *hands* **FIONA** *the green and blue sweater.)*

MAN. Go on.

Scene

> *(We see* **TRISTAN** *on Picture Day.* **FIONA** *tries to get him ready.* **TRISTAN** *uncomfortable.)*

FIONA. Tristan –

> *(***TRISTAN** *fusses loudly.)*

Comb your hair.

> *(***TRISTAN** *fusses again.)*

Fix your shirt.

TRISTAN. No!

FIONA. Tuck it in.
Tuck it in.
Now give me a kiss.
Give me a kiss.

> *(***FIONA** *extracts a kiss from* **TRISTAN.***)*

You look very nice. Now try to keep it that way. Okay?

TRISTAN. I want my book.

FIONA. Well, where'd you put it?

TRISTAN. I want my book.

FIONA. Where did you leave it last?

TRISTAN. I don't know.
I don't know!

FIONA. I'm sorry, honey, but we have to go.

TRISTAN. I want my book!

FIONA. We have to go! C'mon.

> *(***FIONA** *drags* **TRISTAN** *into the school auditorium.)*

TRISTAN. I don't wanna!
I don't wanna!

FIONA. *(to offstage)* Kayla Marie, get down from there –

TRISTAN. *(suddenly)* He doesn't love you. Not even a little.

FIONA. That's not a very nice thing to say, Tris.

TRISTAN. He's gonna leave you.

FIONA. What?

> (**TRISTAN** *returns to what he was before.*)

TRISTAN. I don't wanna!

> (**FIONA** *grabs* **TRISTAN** *by the arm, he goes limp and writhes on the floor. She grabs his arm harder, he writhes more. He flings an arm at her face, she holds his arm.*)

FIONA. Now c'mon.

> (**TRISTAN** *thrashes, she holds him still.* **TRISTAN** *and* **FIONA** *look forward at the unseen Photographer.* **TRISTAN** *embodies the voice of the Photographer, accurate and empty.*)

PHOTOGRAPHER. *Mrs. Hamlin.*

FIONA. Hold on.

PHOTOGRAPHER. *He doesn't have to.*

FIONA. He will. A minute, okay?

Your pants are falling.

Your pants are falling.

Pick up your pants, Tris, they're gonna fall down.

What? You gonna take your picture without your pants?

You want to be the kid without your pants, hm?

What is the matter?

What is the matter with you?

I can't help you if you don't tell me.

I can't make it better if you don't tell me how.

There is nothing wrong with you, Tris.

There is nothing wrong with you that we can't fix.

TRISTAN. Daddy said I'm retarded –

FIONA. He didn't.

TRISTAN. He said I'm hecka mentally challenged.

He said I used to be somebody else's problem.

FIONA. People say lots of things they don't mean.

Now get up.

Get up from the floor, Tris.

Get up from the floor.

TRISTAN. I don't wanna!

> (*FIONA firmly drags* TRISTAN *back into the chair, sits him down.*)

PHOTOGRAPHER. *Eyes nice and wide now.*

MAN. Open your eyes, Fiona.

FIONA. I can't.

> (*The unseen Photographer takes out a comb, combs* TRISTAN*'s hair.*)

TRISTAN. DON'T TOUCH ME!

FIONA. Tristan –

TRISTAN. DON'T TOUCH ME!

FIONA. I'm sorry. He'll be fine.

PHOTOGRAPHER. *Don't sweat it: I used to work with special ed, too.*

FIONA. Oh, no, he's not –

PHOTOGRAPHER. *Eyes nice and wide and –*

> (*Before* FIONA *can respond, there's a camera flash. We see the photograph of* TRISTAN*: dark, scary, off.*)

GUY. Then what?

FIONA. And then we get back to class.

And he knows just the right thing to make a bad day worse.

Someone's mother had brought in cupcakes, a birthday.

> (TRISTAN *pulls out a cupcake.*)

He wouldn't stop screaming until he could have one.
So I let him.
And he pooped in his pants.
I tried to grab him.
He ran away.
So it just slid down his leg,
Brown and sticky.
He didn't even know they were making fun of him.

He thought they were friends.

He thought he had friends.

It made me angry.

I wanted to slap them.

But I couldn't.

Because I only have one child.

And he was covered in shit and cupcake.

So I put him in the car, on newspaper,

And I get a visit and a tree and a Ted.

> *(Next: a summary of her scene with the* **PRINCIPAL***, who also pulls out various objects: a tree, dirty laundry in the course of the scene. He hands them to* **FIONA***. Rotely…)*

PRINCIPAL. Fiona.

FIONA. Ted.

PRINCIPAL. A word?

FIONA. Which word?

PRINCIPAL. Tristan.

FIONA. That word.

PRINCIPAL. More than a word.

Several words.

Two months and three.

Special

Ed

Problem

Child

Joanne

FIONA. *(to us)* That retard.

(to **PRINCIPAL***)* I didn't –

We don't.

PRINCIPAL. Facts and socks.

FIONA. A letter.

PRINCIPAL. A leave.

FIONA. A leaf.
   A tree.

PRINCIPAL. A tree of absence.

FIONA. A lovely parting gift.

PRINCIPAL. Just for now.
   Leafed off.

FIONA. Fuck off.

PRINCIPAL. Fiona, please.

FIONA. How long?

PRINCIPAL. Six months.
   Foot and a half.
   Maybe something good'll grow,
   Just not your kid.

FIONA. Happy Picture Day,
   You asshat.

   (The **PRINCIPAL** *disappears.)*

   And I got back in the car and I left.
   I drove.
   He sat.
   He sat picking shit off his legs and into his hair.
   I told him to stop.
   I told him – *(stops)* Nothing.
   I told him –

MAN. Nothing?

FIONA. I told him –
   Now sit still.

MAN. *(as* **FIONA***)* "Now sit still, you move one more inch
   and I'm getting the yardstick. We get home, and I am
   getting the yardstick!"

FIONA. I didn't say that.

MAN. No?

FIONA. I didn't say it like that.
   I didn't want to hurt him.
   I just wanted to scare him.

I couldn't find the napkins.

It was soaking through the newspaper,

Onto my new car smell.

He was right under my nose and he stank.

He was right under my nose and I wanted him anywhere else but there.

I tried to find something that might make him better, might make him clean.

So I pull over

To where the trees meet the road

And I turn off into a gas station –

(**TRISTAN** *in the car.*)

TRISTAN. For gas?

FIONA. No.

TRISTAN. For candy?

FIONA. No.

TRISTAN. Then what?

FIONA. Nothing.

TRISTAN. We're going in for nothing?

FIONA. Yes.

TRISTAN. I want some.

FIONA. No.

TRISTAN. I want nothing.

I want some nothing!

FIONA. Keep it up and you're gonna get nothing.

(**FIONA** *opens the car door.* **TRISTAN** *squirms: the bathroom dance.*)

TRISTAN. I have to go.

FIONA. You just went.

(**TRISTAN** *squirms more.*)

TRISTAN. I have to go.

I HAVE TO GO.

FIONA. You go when you get home. You get home in five
    minutes.

    You can't wait five minutes?

TRISTAN. I HAVE TO GO!

FIONA. I'll be back in a minute.

    Now sit up.

    Now lock the door.

    Now stay inside.

> *(As soon as* FIONA *turns her back,* TRISTAN
> *transforms into the* MAN*.)*

MAN. Now turn your back.

    Now walk away.

    Now make a wish.

    And tell me –

> *(*FIONA *hears the* MAN*, but doesn't turn around.)*

FIONA. Yes?

MAN. How long does it take to lose a child?

FIONA. Who are you?

MAN. I was right under your nose.

FIONA. Wait.

MAN. Didn't you hear?

    I have to go.

    (as TRISTAN*)* I have to go!

> *(Without turning,* FIONA *continues to walk away.)*

FIONA. I went in and got myself a Kit Kat,

    And instead of coming right back,

    I go the other way,

    Around the corner

    Out of view

    Out of sight

    Out of mind

    Out of my hair for just a minute

    A moment

A pause

A beat

A breath

> *(Everyone breathes, exhales.)*

An eternity.

> *(**FIONA** has a Kit Kat. She ducks around a corner, out of **TRISTAN**'s view, and eats it. The chocolate gets on her hands, her mouth. She licks her fingers, savors.)*

And I hear the sound of a car door opening.

And I hear him say –

MAN. What?

FIONA. "Something."

I hear him say something, so I do nothing.

I just stand there and hope he doesn't find me.

But when I come back, the door is open.

I tear into the car

And there it is,

In the back

Under the blanket

There it is, his book,

Right where I left it.

And out of the corner of my eye,

Between the road and the trees and a mouth full of chocolate,

I think I see something –

Something like –

MAN. A blue Honda

A red Civic

A black SUV with the windows tinted

A '94 Camero with the radio on

And a sticker on the bumper:

"Kiss Me, I'm Irish."

"Ithaca is Gorges."

MAN. *(cont.)* "New Jersey is for Pedophiles."

"Kiss Me, I'm Gorgeous."

"Kiss Me, I'm Gone."

I'm outta here.

FIONA. But I turn around.

The ground is slick with shit.

I bang my hip.

I stub my toe.

And I get back up.

And by then, nothing.

Nothing on my hands but guilt and chocolate,

Brown and sticky.

And I wait for a voice over the loudspeaker to let me know:

LOUDSPEAKER. "Will the owner of a black SUV"

"Of a small blue boy"

"Of a green and blue sweater"

"Come up to the front?"

"We have your child and he's a sweater."

"We have your son, may he rest in pieces."

FIONA. But all I get is someone's voice telling me:

> *(The following is spoken as normally as possible, even if there is constant revision and rewinding of the dialogue. The voice is kind, gentle.* FIONA *as the* OFFICER…)

Mrs. Hamlin?

Can you hear me?

If you hear me,

Tell me what I'm saying.

What I'm saying is

Would you like a seat?

Would you like a

Wouldn't you like to know

Where he is.

Where is he?
Can I get you anything?
I can get you anything except your
Husband? Do you have a husband I should
I should call your husband.
Is there anything you want to tell him?
We don't have to –
But we should.

(Back to FIONA*'s perspective. She addresses us.)*

And you realize:
Life is just a series of
We don't have to
But we should.
We might as well
As we can,
Don't you think?
You don't think.
You just stumble.
'Cause in times like this
Words fail me.
Like they just stop trying
Like whatever they were doing before
They don't now.
Like they just don't even seem to –

(The MAN *comes into view. He is now the* OFFICER.*)*

OFFICER. – hear me?
Mrs. Hamlin?
Can you hear me?
Can I get you anything you don't have anymore?
Mrs. Hamlin?
If you hear me

OFFICER & FIONA. Tell me what I'm saying
What I'm saying is

OFFICER. Within the first forty-eight hours, ninety percent
of missing children are found.

Seventy percent of the time, it's just miscommunication.

A car can travel up to a hundred-twenty miles an hour.

An ant can lift fifty times its own weight.

Cats can fall ten stories and survive.

Dogs can tell when you've lied to them.

The human body can survive five days without water

Three weeks without food

And years without love.

We are amazing.

We are brilliant.

We are what we make of it.

What I'm saying is:

Nine times out of ten, they're at home, at a neighbor's

– undercover, underground –

– under a porch, at a friend's, hanging out –

– hanging from –

What I'm saying is

Nine times out of ten:

In the time it takes for a missing child to be reported

For the human body to decompose

For lungs to stop

Hearts to break

Ashes to ashes

And sons to dust:

We've usually located the kid.

So worst case scenario is –

OFFICER/FIONA. – this is it.

> *(The **OFFICER** disappears.)*

> *(**FIONA** back in the present with **GUY**.)*

FIONA. And in the space between my heart and my lungs

Between a beat and a breath,

It hits you,

Meaning it occurs to you like a ton of bricks:

Worse case scenario is, this is it.

Just me, myself, and Guy:

Nobody here but us chickens,

We cowards.

Worse case scenario is: he was right under my nose and I lost him.

GUY. And why can't you just say that?

FIONA. People want a story.

You only get one story.

You can't say:

I hit him

And

I loved him

And

He was sweet

And

He was spoiled

And

Sometimes I wished he was something other than what he was.

And

He'd yell

And

He'd kick

And

Sometimes I wasn't even sure he loved me, not even a little.

People want black and white

And all I've got is

Green and blue

Black and tan

Red and white with stripes all over.

Brown and sticky.

You know how long it takes to lose a child?

GUY. I know.

FIONA. No, you don't. You want to. You try to. But you
    don't.

    Because you didn't.

GUY. Then tell me.

FIONA. It's the time it takes to turn around

    Slip on shit.

    Bang your hip.

    Stub your toe.

    And get back up.

    Three minutes.

    And this is something I just can't get over.

GUY. What you can't get over –

FIONA. " – you go through." I know.

    But every day, I wake up and I see no way through. I see
    no way over or under or around or through.

    All I see is something we've gotten ourselves into that
    we can never get out of.

    I close my eyes and all I see are cantaloupes and can't-
    escapes and can't-even-sleep-at-nights.

    I close my eyes and all I hear is –

MAN. *(as **PRINCIPAL**)* Tristan. It's about Tristan.

    *(as **DETECTIVE**)* More than enough guilt to go around!

    *(as **MAN**)* Take care of your things, or you're gonna lose
    them.

    *(The **MAN** disappears.)*

FIONA. In a word, he's gone.

    And I need him, guy.

    I need him like I need a hole in my head.

FIONA. *(cont.)* Like I need a mouth to breathe.

    I need to find who did it.

    'Cause if I can't get justice, it's just us –

    (corrects) Just me.

GUY. Even if we never get justice, we can still get dinner.

FIONA. Guy –

GUY. And better. We'll get better.

FIONA. But then what?

GUY. Then we'll get coffee –

FIONA. And dessert?

GUY. And dessert.

We'll get home.

We'll get sleep.

We'll get up.

We'll get going.

We'll get away.

We'll get by.

We'll get back.

We'll get fat.

We'll get ulcers.

We'll get older.

We'll get wiser.

And even if we never get over, at least we'll get through.

FIONA. How long will that take?

GUY. Three minutes. Six months. Foot and a half.

We'll go outside, we'll plant ourselves.

And maybe something good will grow.

FIONA. I guess. I hope.

> (GUY *finds the Picture Day photographs in the case file, holds them for* FIONA *to see.* FIONA *considers it.*)

> (GUY *offers a hand to* FIONA. *They link fingers.* FIONA *edges towards* GUY, *the chasm between them on the couch closes a little.*)

> (*A noise. The sound of a branch hitting a window. Or the wind blowing a door closed.*)

> (*Behind them,* TRISTAN *appears.*)

GUY. You hear something?

FIONA. No. Just a tree. Probably just a tree.

> (*FIONA and GUY look forward at a photograph.*)

GUY. So what do you think?

FIONA. It's okay.

> (*Camera flash. An awkward but okay family portrait.*)

It'll be okay.

> (*The family portrait fades out, lights down.*)

> (*Curtain.*)